Mish*mash*

Mishmash

by Molly Cone / Illustrated by Leonard Shortall

Houghton Mifflin Company Boston

To Gary in memory of his dog Tiny

Mish*mash*

1

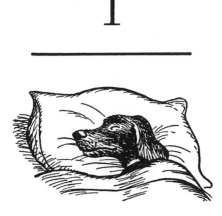

"I DON'T FEEL too hungry," Pete said that morning to no one in particular. And he wondered if he should have spoken a little louder, for no one in particular paid much attention to what he said.

His father glanced up from the pages of the morning newspaper with a cheerful look. His mother, stirring cereal in the top of the double boiler, looked cheerful too. But some people just never feel very cheerful first thing in the morning, and this morning Pete was one of them. He frowned.

"Now all you have to do," said his mother, placing a bowl of cereal before him, "is take your last year's report card to the fifth grade teacher in Room 41. That's all you have to do." She filled a pitcher with milk and set it before him. "There is a little girl about your age next door," she said sounding as if this should make up for there being no boys his age in this new neighborhood.

It occurred to Pete that he didn't know anybody at all in this new school, and the thought made his throat prickly. Pete gulped, remembering suddenly that he had lost his breakfast the day he started school in the first grade. And although that had happened long ago, Pete pushed his chair back. He had a strange feeling that it might happen all over again. His face got red at just the thought of it.

His father rattled the newspaper. "Well, listen to this!" he said, and read to them from it. "Wanted — a good home for puppies — 616 Spring Street." He looked out the window. "That would be six blocks past the school, I would imagine," he guessed.

For the moment Pete forgot about his stomach.

"You mean I can have one?" he said, not really believing it. He had always wished for a dog. They had talked about getting a dog the way they had talked about moving out of the apartment and into a house of their own. He hadn't really expected any of it to even happen.

"Well I don't see why not," said Mr. Peters.

Mrs. Peters said, "You can go to see them after school."

Pete finished his breakfast in a hurry. He tore the ad from the paper and put the clipping in his pocket, took his report card and his lunch sack and opened the back door.

Pete slammed the door behind him just as the girl next door appeared on her front steps. He pretended not to see her. Quickly he ran down the walk and turned toward the school. He walked briskly, with his hands stuck in his pockets, as if he didn't think it was much of anything to be going to a new school. "Dog — dog — I'm going to get a dog," he whispered resolutely to himself, keeping his mind on that. In spite of this, his legs began to move more slowly. He was aware suddenly of the girl behind him who began to walk more slowly too.

Too slowly he thought. He hastened his step, and by the sound of the quickening of footsteps behind him, he knew that she had begun to walk faster too. Pete scowled. When he began to walk faster, so did she. When he slowed down, she did too.

4

He stopped suddenly, and bent low to untie and retie his shoelace. This would give her a chance to walk on ahead, he thought. But the girl behind him stopped too. Wrathfully he turned upon her.

"You stop that!" he ordered.

She looked back at him innocently. "Stop what?" she said.

"You stop following me!" he said and flushed, for he knew at once how silly that sounded.

She giggled. "I'm not following you; I'm walking to school. I always walk to school this way. It's the only way you can get there."

Pete grunted, turned about and hurried on, trying to ignore her. But he couldn't ignore the sound of feet merely three paces behind, matching his own, step for step, fast or slow, long or short. As they neared the school Pete became aware that a good many of these other kids noticed it too. His cheeks felt uncomfortably hot, and his ears burned. Hatred of this girl at his heels filled him. He hated her and he hated this school, and he hated the kids — and he entered Room 41, placed his report card on the teacher's desk, and took a seat in the fifth row.

He thought about his dog. He decided it wouldn't make any difference that he had no friends. His best friend would be his dog. He and his dog would go everywhere together. It made a pleasant picture in his mind, himself and his dog. It made such a pleasant picture that he had no idea his smile was coming through until he realized he was sitting there staring at the teacher with the smile on his face. Quickly Pete looked down at his hands. When he glanced up again, the teacher was looking the other way.

The bell rang, but no one paid any attention. One boy was chewing gum. It made a loud pop as he blew it out into a bubble and he crossed his eyes before it broke. The girls giggled. Pete looked at the teacher. She too was watching the boy.

"Good morning, John Williams," she said.

John Williams, with the surprise showing on his face at the teacher's knowing his name, hastily removed the gum from his mouth and parked it behind his ear. "Mornin'," he mumbled and slouched back in his seat and looked at his thumbs.

"We don't chew gum during school hours," she said to everyone. "That is," she amended, "unless you are ready to stand treat for the whole class."

The children gazed at her in disbelief.

"John Williams," she said, "did you bring enough gum to share with the whole class?"

John ducked his head even lower.

"In that case," the teacher said calmly, "will you please change the parking place of your gum" — and she picked up the wastebasket and held it in front of her.

John inched himself out of his seat and slowly went down the aisle. The teacher waited politely. The boy took the gum from behind his ear and dropped it into the wastebasket. There was a sharp ping as it hit the metal.

The class laughed. Even John Williams laughed. And the teacher didn't try to hide her smile this time. She laughed out loud with the rest of them.

Pete looked at her curiously. Her teeth stuck out in a friendly way when she laughed, and when she spoke, her voice was loud and clear. She didn't seem to be afraid of anybody. She was certainly different from any teacher he had ever had.

"This is the fifth grade room in the Ridge View Elementary School, in the city of Tacoma, state of Washington, U.S.A.," she announced, and looked carefully around the room before she explained: "Once a third grader wandered in the first day by mistake, so now I always make sure we are all where we want to be."

Pete looked, too, turning his head one way, and then the other. Everybody looked at everybody else, smiling.

"I am going to introduce myself," the teacher continued, "and then we will start with the first seat on the left, and each of you will rise, give the class your name, number of brothers and sisters, mention your favorite games, hobbies or pets. In this way we will quickly become acquainted. "My name is Winifred Patch." She turned and wrote *Miss Patch* on the blackboard. She wrote fast and big, crossed the t with a swift stroke, and turned again to the class.

"I have one brother and five sisters," she said. "I like horses and dogs, rainy weather and angel food cake!" Her smile was so broad that everybody smiled with her. She nodded to the boy in the first seat.

The boy stood up. "My name is Anthony Hardy. I have two sisters, three goldfish and a hamster. My hobby is my hamster." He sat down.

Pete hardly listened as the others rose, one by one. He sat very straight with his hands clasped, practicing what he was going to say. At last it was his turn. He stood up, as each of the others had done.

"My name is John Peters," he said, "but my father's name is John, too, so I'm called Pete. I have no brothers or sisters — but I have a dog!" And he sat down. His heart was beating rapidly.

He didn't have a dog yet, of course, but he would have soon. Just as soon as school let out. He figured that was close enough.

"Pete Peters." Miss Patch repeated his name as if she liked the sound of it. "My brother's name is Pete. I always called him my favorite brother. Of course I had only one brother." She winked at the class. "My family was always long on girls."

Pete suddenly felt very close to Miss Patch. Almost as if they were related.

"I collect rocks," said John Williams who was next. He spoke loudly. Pete smiled smugly to himself. Old John was just jealous because the teacher's favorite brother wasn't called John. "I've got two little brothers."

"Huh," a girl said. "We've got a whole pile of rocks out behind our house."

"Rock collecting is a very interesting hobby," said Miss Patch. "The earth is made of many different layers of rocks. Some day we'll ask John Williams to bring some of his specimens to show."

John sat down beaming. Pete wished, suddenly,

that he had a collection of something.

The next boy who stood up merely gave his name and sat down.

"No brothers or sisters?" asked Miss Patch curiously.

As the boy shook his head, Miss Patch queried, "No hobbies?"

And again the boy shook his head.

"Well, perhaps you will tell us, then, what you did this summer."

"Nothing," said the boy. "I didn't have time to do anything. I had to help my dad build a room onto our house."

Miss Patch raised her eyebrows and looked around at the class. "This boy builds a room onto his house and calls that nothing! Well, I call that something!"

Pete wished suddenly that he had helped his father build their house. He felt a little bit ashamed that they had bought their house already built.

Pete ate his lunch by himself, thinking mostly about the dog. After lunch he followed the others back into the room. The boy who had helped his father build a room onto his house placed a large cooky half wrapped in a paper napkin on the teacher's desk.

"Oh!" said Miss Patch, as if she were not used to receiving presents. "Is this part of your lunch?"

The boy shook his head. "That was extra," he said offhandedly.

"Well I thank you, Ralph!" she said. "If you're sure it is extra I'll save it for my after-school snack."

A couple of the boys snickered. Ralph's face grew red. He sat down in his seat, and then turned his head to the boys behind him, shielding his mouth with his hand. "I didn't really want it," he whispered. "Tastes like poison!" And he grimaced.

But he didn't fool anybody, Pete thought. Not anybody at all. Pete wished he had saved the cooky in his lunch for the teacher.

The afternoon went too fast. Pete raised his arm high when Miss Patch asked for a volunteer to take a message to the office, and again when she needed a boy to help unroll maps. But although her glance rested on him lightly each time, she chose someone else. Pete wished he had chosen the first seat in the first row instead of the last seat in the fifth row. When the bell rang at the close of the afternoon session, everyone was surprised.

"Oh!" said Miss Patch. "Is it that time already?"

Then she rapped on the desk three times with her pencil for attention. "Every night I choose a room helper," she explained, "to clean the blackboard, empty the wastebasket and help check out."

Her glance traveled around the room, and every girl and boy sat up very straight and turned their eyes to the teacher.

Pete sat up particularly straight. He knew she was going to choose him. He just knew it. He tried to control the smile that was already stretching his lips.

"Wanda Sparling," said Miss Patch. "It would give me great pleasure if you would be my room helper tonight."

Swallowing his disappointment, Pete turned

13

curiously to the back of the room to see who Wanda Sparling was. Wanda Sparling stood up grinning. Pete frowned. Wanda Sparling was the girl next door! He watched her walk importantly down the aisle. He remembered how she had followed on his heels to school; and he stuck out his foot.

"Ouch!" he said as she trod on it.

Pete pulled in his feet. He hated her all over again.

2

PETE walked down Spring Street looking for the
address in the advertisement he was holding. It
was a mixed-up street. First there was a gas station, then an empty lot with a shack on it, then a
house with the windows boarded up, and then a
tiny yard with a short white fence around it and a
walk lined with flowers and at the end of the walk
sat a little red house-trailer, with smoke coming out
of the chimney. Pete stopped and looked at his
clipping. This was it all right!

He went up the walk and knocked lightly on
the door of the little house on wheels. While he
waited he looked all around the yard. There were

no signs of any dogs that he could see. But then he guessed they might be inside.

"Come in!" a voice shouted.

Pete stepped back a bit at the sound of it. It was a very loud voice. Gingerly he put his hand on the doorknob and turned it. The door stuck, so he pushed hard. It flew open and Pete fell in. He blinked as he closed the door behind him.

Sitting not three feet from the door was an old man with the end of a cigar in his mouth. He was sitting on a built-in bench and leaning his elbows on a built-in table, and he was making marks on a map.

"Come in," said the man without taking the cigar out of his mouth. "Come in . . . come in."

"I'm already in," said Pete politely.

At the sound of Pete's voice, the old man looked up. He chuckled. "Well, so you are," he said. "Well, now you're in, what's on your mind?"

Pete swallowed. He placed the newspaper advertisement on the desk. "I came for one of the puppies," he said.

"No puppies here," said the man.

"But it says . . ." began Pete, wondering if he had the right address.

"Maybe I should say," said the man, "there aren't any puppies here any more. Gone!" he said. "All gone!" The old man moved his cigar from one side of his mouth to the other. "As a matter of fact," he said, "the last one was picked up two days ago."

"Two days ago!" Pete looked at the newspaper in his hand.

"Oh, the ad ran in the paper this morning all right," said the man. "Special rate. Three days for the price of one," he said. "I figured I might as well get my money's worth." Then he laughed to himself as if he had said something funny.

"You mean I'm too late for a puppy?" asked Pete. It was necessary to blink his eyes all of a sudden. Maybe it was that old cigar smoke or something. He brushed his arms across his eyes.

The old man looked at him closely. "You want a dog? Is that right, boy?"

"I never had a dog," said Pete, feeling terribly sorry for himself. "We always lived in an apartment before."

"Hmmm," said the man. "And your mom and dad sent you out to get yourself a dog, did they?"

At Pete's nod, the old man slapped his hand on his knee. "Might be we can fix you up after all. But he's no puppy!" said the old man warningly.

The old man picked up a cane and poked at the door. He leaned across the table. "Mish!" he shouted. "His name is Mishmash," he said over his shoulder to Pete, and smiled at his private joke.

Pete heard a scrambling and before he could step out of the way, a large black hound hurtled through the doorway, yipping and yapping joyously. He clambered around Pete, clumsily stepping on Pete's toes, almost knocking him over in his effort to welcome him.

"He's certainly friendly," said Pete, stepping back a little as the dog almost pushed him over in its exuberance.

"You've put your finger on it, boy," said the

man, as if Pete had said something profound. "Friendly is the word. Why he's about the most friendly dog you'll ever hope to find."

Pete laughed. "Whoa, Mish," he said, "down dog. Good dog. Good Mish." He patted Mish's black face. "My dad had a black dog when he was a kid." He was unable to keep the excitement out of his voice. This was a dog! This was a real dog!

Suddenly he straightened up. "We've got a new house," he said, thinking of those gleaming floors. "Will he — does he — "

"Oh, pshaw!" said the man. "He's a perfect gentleman, he is." Then the man winked. "Born and bred in a palace, I'll have you know."

In spite of himself Pete was impressed.

"Well," said the man, "It was really a hotel — big as a palace — called the Palace Hotel." And this time when he laughed Pete could smile with him.

"Don't you worry about him, boy," said the man. "Take my word for it. You don't have to worry about him!"

Pete couldn't help it. He bent down and hugged Mish. And when he straightened up, the dog stood up on his hind legs, put his paws on Pete's shoulders, and slathered Pete's face with his tongue. Pete laughed. The dog liked him!

"Well, he certainly has taken to you," said the man, as if he couldn't believe his eyes.

Pete tried to hide his pride. "Down Mish," he said firmly. "Down boy."

Pete wondered how the old man could bear to give up such a fine dog as Mish.

"If he were my dog, I wouldn't give him away," Pete said.

The old man sighed. "Well, kid, it's this way. I'm getting old, I am." He raised his arm.

Pete gazed at the shaking hand and nodded sympathetically.

"That Mish is just too young a dog to be saddled with an old man like me. What he needs is someone lively." With the back of his hand the old man tapped Pete's shoulder. "Someone who takes to him."

"I like him," Pete said quickly. "I do like him."

"He's not the kind of dog you can give to just anybody," the man said, scratching his chin and looking at Pete closely.

Pete drew himself up. He tried to look like somebody. Somebody you could give this kind of a dog to.

The man nodded then as if he had come to a decision.

"Goodbye, Mish," said the man. He patted the dog's head vigorously . . . so vigorously that Mish ducked and eased over to Pete.

The old man sighed. "See, he's yours already. Well, that's life, I guess!"

Pete walked down the brick path and out the little white gate with Mish trotting at his heels. It felt good to have the black hound walking along beside him. He could just see himself coming home from school each day with Mish scrambling to greet him. He could see himself sitting there at the dining-room table doing his lesson, with Mish sitting at his feet, his chin resting faithfully on

Pete's shoe. He could see his mother and his father and himself and Mish standing there in the firelight — just like a Christmas card.

When they reached the intersection, Pete grasped Mish's collar firmly. He wasn't going to let anything happen to his dog. They reached the other curb safely and then he let Mish prance onward. In front of his house stood Wanda Sparling, watching their approach with interest.

"Be careful!" Pete warned her sharply. "He doesn't much like girls."

Wanda sniffed. "Here doggie," she said, "nice doggie." Mish bounded over to her and licked her outstretched hand with his wet tongue. Wanda giggled. "Not much he doesn't like girls. Not much I'd say."

Pete whistled and Mish ignored it. Pete grasped his collar firmly. He couldn't have hated Wanda more. "You'd better go play with your dolls," he ordered. "If I hadn't called him off, he might of chomped your hand off — right up to here." He brought his free hand down sharply at his elbow.

Wanda giggled. "There's nothing about you, Pete Peters," she said calmly, "that I like" — she grinned impishly — "except maybe your dog." She turned and walked importantly away from him.

"Well you just stay away from him, Wanda Sparling. You hear me? You stay away from him — for your own good!"

Wanda turned. She smiled sweetly. "I'm not going to stay away from him at all," she stated. " 'Cause I don't have to be afraid of him. 'Cause you wouldn't let him hurt me, would you, Pete Peters?" Her voice changed suddenly from sugar and spice to a screech and a yell. "Because if you did," she hollered, "my dad would break every bone in your body!" And she banged the screen door behind her.

Pete patted Mish's head and regarded him proudly. He wondered what his father would say when he saw Mish — he just wondered!

3

"GOOD HEAVENS!" said his father. "You call that a puppy!"

"As I told Mom," said Pete patiently. "He was out of puppies."

"Hmmmm," said Mr. Peters, looking at his wife.

Pete's mother said hastily, "Don't look at me. It wasn't *my* idea," she added pointedly.

Pete's father grunted. "Where's he going to sleep?" he asked.

"In my room?" said Pete hopefully.

"In the basement," said his mother firmly.

"Ah, gee whiz, Mom," said Pete. "I bet he's never slept in a basement in his life."

"We'll put a nice big box down next to the furnace, with a nice soft blanket in it . . ." His mother stopped suddenly. Pete looked at her, and then followed her gaze.

There was Mish — padding up the carpeted hall. He went up the three steps, turned, and stopped in front of Pete's bedroom door. He looked back at them. And as Pete made no move to join him, he went on in. They heard the soft thud as he jumped from the floor to the bed.

"Well!" said Mr. Peters.

"He wants to sleep with me!" said Pete, pleased that Mish had taken matters into his own hands — or paws.

Pete's mother lifted her chin. "We'll put a big box down next to the furnace with a nice soft blanket in it," she said again, but this time there was a firmness that Pete could not mistake.

He looked imploringly at her. And she returned his gaze steadfastly.

Pete's father cleared his throat. "Why don't we," he said brightly, "put a nice big box down next to the furnace and put a nice soft blanket in it — right now?" Then he opened the basement door.

Disconsolately Pete followed his father down the basement steps. He stood with a long face while his father dug through the packing boxes and found a big crate. He stuck his thumbs in his pockets and waited, disapprovingly silent, while his father knocked one of the sides off the crate.

"Mish will be tickled pink with this," said his father, pushing the three-sided box into the corner near the furnace.

Pete looked doubtful. "He's not used to sleeping by himself," he pointed out.

"Now look here, son," said Pete's father. He put his hand on Pete's shoulder. But what he was going to say Pete never found out, for at that moment the bell rang — two notes at the front door. And at the sound of the bell, they heard a scuffling, sliding sound from the bedroom and a yip-yelping as Mish streaked down the hallway.

Both Pete and his father made a dash for the

stairway. They gained the top just as Pete's mother opened the front door, but it was Mish who welcomed the guest. Tail wagging, tongue hanging, throat yipping in joyous greeting, he bounded out.

"Down, Mish!" said Pete and his mother and his father at once and together.

Pete grasped hold of Mish's collar as the man stepped back so hastily that he fell over the planter box.

"Friendly little mutt, isn't he?" said the man, picking himself up. But he sounded doubtful, then scribbled something on a pink paper and handed it to Mrs. Peters.

"Your oil man," he said. "I just filled the tank."

"Thank you," said Mrs. Peters, and closed the door after him. She stood there a moment with her hand on the doorknob, frowning, her eyes on Mish. She sighed. Then she just went into the kitchen and began to put the dishes into the dishwasher.

Pete's father opened his mouth, but all that

came out was a sigh. Then he turned and went on into the living room where he sat down in the biggest, softest chair and put the evening newspaper over his face.

Pete followed Mish back up the three steps into the bedroom. He closed the door. Mish jumped on the bed again and curled up and closed his eyes. Then he opened one eye to look at Pete.

Pete laughed. He flopped down on the bed and put his arms around Mish. "*I* like you, Mish," he said. "I really do!"

Pete didn't fall asleep immediately that night. He lay on his back, his hands behind his head, listening to the scuffling sounds in the basement. It sounded to him as if Mish didn't like his nice big box down there. It sounded as if he was re-arranging things to his liking.

Pete didn't know how much later it was when he opened his eyes in the darkness to hear odd sounds under the floor. He raised himself on one elbow and listened. It sounded as if Mish was hammering on the basement door with both paws.

He heard his father roar, "Mish! Quiet!"

His mother said, "For heaven's sake, what are you yelling at?" His father muttered something about the basement door. "Well, I locked it myself," said his mother.

For a time Mish stopped doing whatever he was doing at the basement door.

Pete's eyes had just fallen shut again when he came instantly wide awake. For Mish was barking. Pete could hear him running up and down the basement steps and barking.

He heard a stirring from his mother's and father's room. He heard his father pad down the hallway. And then Pete fell asleep again. It seemed to him that he intermittently woke and slept the whole night through. But he figured he must have really been asleep all the time. For when he awoke in the morning, Mish was curled up on the pillow beside him — his black face as innocent as a baby's.

4

PETE looked at the clock on his desk. It was time to get up. He sniffed. The whole house seemed deep in slumber. He sniffed again. But there were no breakfast smells floating from the kitchen. He sat up.

His father came down the hallway and peered sleepily into Pete's room. He yawned. "Morning, Pete," he said then. Then he slipped a tie under his collar and began to twist a knot into it.

Pete jumped out of bed. "Where's Mom?"

"Asleep!" said his father. And his voice was suddenly stern. "And everybody around here had better be quiet this morning because I don't intend to wake her up to fix anybody's breakfast." He gazed sternly at Mish, and Mish, his eyes still closed, wagged his tail. Pete began to pull on his clothes. "I'll be glad to fix breakfast," he said.

His father looked at the watch on his wrist. "Thanks, son," he said, "but I have a breakfast meeting downtown. Just fix it for yourself, get yourself off to school and let your mother sleep."

"Okay," said Pete. He raised his head from tying his shoe and looked at Mish. He just couldn't tell about Mish. Mish didn't seem to know how to be quiet.

"Tie Mish to the clothesline outside when you leave," said his father, and walked briskly down the hall.

"I don't think he is going to like being tied up," said Pete doubtfully, but his father had already closed the front door behind him.

Thoughtfully he went about preparing his own breakfast. His mother was still asleep. He listened, feeling a little guilty, hoping he could get out without waking her up.

He filled a bowl with dry cereal and poured a glass of milk, and set these on the kitchen table. Then he rinsed out the old chipped bowl his mother had given him yesterday for Mish, filled it generously with dog food and set it on the kitchen floor. Mish sniffed at it, walked around it, sniffed at it again. Then he sat there looking at Pete.

"It's good! Mish, old boy," said Pete. He put two slices of bread in the toaster. When he turned around, Mish was sitting on Pete's chair, eating from Pete's bowl of cereal.

Pete helped himself to another bowl of cereal, placed it on the other side of the table, and sat there, facing Mish companionably, rather pleased to have someone to breakfast with.

Mish, after he had eaten, licked his cereal bowl clean, burped lightly, jumped down and stepped across to the back door. He raised one paw and batted at the doorknob. Pete got up and opened the back door for him.

When Pete slipped into his seat at school that morning, he noticed the orange immediately. A round, large, thick-skinned orange was placed on the middle of Miss Patch's desk. He felt a sudden sharp twinge. He wished it had been he who had thought to bring an orange to Miss Patch. There was a bowl of these same big oranges on the kitchen counter — only he just hadn't thought of it. He slumped down in his seat. It would have been so easy to put an orange in his pocket and bring it to school. He wished he had done it.

Miss Patch came in. The class laughed when she stopped suddenly at the sight of the orange. She walked slowly to the desk. She folded her arms around herself and walked around her desk.

"My goodness," she said then. "For a moment I thought it wasn't real." She picked it up. She tossed it into the air and caught it. "It is real!" she said. The class laughed again.

"Now I wonder who it was," she said, "who put it there." Pete looked around. Everyone else looked around, too.

The teacher looked about in surprise. No one said a word.

"Hmmm," she said, looking about. "I wonder . . . it couldn't have been you, could it, Pete?" she said, with a smile.

Pete folded his hands on his desk. He was perfectly honest. "Well," he said, wishing he could tell her that he wished it had been him, "it could have . . ." he said.

There was a sudden shrill treble from the back of the room. "Well, it wasn't!"

Everyone turned around. Wanda Sparling had risen to her feet. Her chin thrust out, her dark eyes turned beady. Wanda put her hands on her hips. "It wasn't him at all," she shouted. "It was me!"

The class was suddenly still, in surprise.

Pete turned all the way around. "I didn't say it

was me!" he hollered back at her. "I just said it
could have been!"

"Well, it wasn't!" Wanda shrieked.

The whole class turned to the teacher. Miss
Patch stood there, the orange sitting on the palm
of one hand.

"Thank you very much, Wanda," she said, just
as if there had been no rumpus at all. "I do think,"
she said, "this is the biggest orange I have ever
seen." And she set it down on the corner of the

desk. "And now let's all turn to page 4 in our new language art books and read our spelling story."

Pete bent his head over the pages of his book. He decided Wanda Sparling was about the ugliest girl he'd ever seen. He decided if he ever had a birthday party, there was one person he wouldn't invite — and that was Wanda Sparling. He spent so much energy hating Wanda Sparling that when Miss Patch called time for testing he realized that he hadn't studied the words at all. His eye scanned the list hurriedly. He was one of the last in the room to close his book and he did so reluctantly.

Miss Patch sat at her desk and looked thoughtfully around the room, her chin in her hand. "Why don't we, just for fun, have an old-fashioned spelling bee?" She looked questioningly at the class.

"Yeah!" said the class.

Miss Patch stood up. "Girls line up on one side of the room, boys on the other." She clasped her hands. "Scat!" she said.

The girls made a rush for one side, the boys for

the other. Pete gained his place without difficulty, not too close to one end, not too close to the other. He shifted his feet, feeling uneasy. He wished he had paid more attention to the words. He tried to remember what he had seen on the printed page, but, unaccountably, he couldn't remember any words — not a one. He swallowed. He had always been a 100 per cent speller in the fourth grade. His mother had always been so proud of those 100 per cent papers he brought home. "Well, one thing you are," he could hear her say with satisfaction, "is a *good* speller." And the peculiar emphasis she put on good made it sound as if this was a talent like singing, maybe, or violin playing.

Miss Patch opened her book. She smiled.

"Joan," she said to the first girl in the row of girls, "we will start out with you. Spell" — she glanced at her book, and an intent, almost pained, expression settled on Joan's face.

"View," said Miss Patch. "Look out the window at the lovely view."

Automatically all heads turned to the window. The courtyard was empty. Across the court, in the kindergarten section, the children were standing beside their desks with their arms stretched up. Little kids. Miss Patch's class smiled. They felt very old, and grown up, and Joan spelled "view," putting the "i" before the "e" where it belonged. There was a sigh of relief from the girls' side.

Miss Patch said, "Steeple." She said, thought-fully, "The church I like best has a little wooden steeple." The first boy spelled "steeple" correctly.

"Friends," said Miss Patch, looking meaning-fully, first at Wanda and then at Pete. "Boys and girls in this class should be friends." Wanda stared pointedly over Pete's head, and Pete made a face. He had no intention of being friends with any girl — particularly not *this* one.

The words went back and forth like a ping-pong ball — to the boys — then to the girls. John Williams missed "autumn" and Janey Lander put the "n" on, and scored a lead for the girls' side. Then Wanda Sparling hesitated on the word "slight."

It was a triumph for Pete. He could have spelled it backwards. It was a fourth grade word — he didn't even have to study it. "S-l-i-g-h-t," he spelled loudly, with justifiable pride.

"Correct!" said Miss Patch, and closed her spelling book.

"It's a tie," she announced, "and high time we begin our arithmetic."

With his hands in his pockets, Pete strolled to his seat. He figured he had shown that Wanda Sparling where he stood. And he put his whole attention on his arithmetic book.

Well — almost his whole attention. He glanced now and then at Miss Patch. He hoped she would notice how earnestly he was studying. He wondered if he really reminded her of her favorite brother. He certainly hoped so.

The day rolled by. At recess Miss Patch showed that she could pitch a ball better than any boy in the fifth grade. In gym, when she led the class in square dancing, she hollered right out above the music, loud and clear, and took Pete as a partner and danced right along with the rest of them. When they formed a big circle, she joined in and did the hokey-pokey as vigorously as any of them.

Back in his seat in the classroom, doing the next day's arithmetic, Pete sighed and allowed his eyes to rest fondly on Miss Patch. His glance drifted to the big clock on the side wall. The big hand pointed to twelve; the little hand to three. Pete took a deep breath and turned his eyes again to Miss Patch's face. He folded his hands over his completed arithmetic paper. Then he held his breath as Miss Patch raised her head, looked briefly at him and tapped with her pencil three times on the edge of the desk.

Pete's heart lifted. He sat motionless looking at the clock. Yesterday at three Miss Patch had chosen her after-school room helper. Pete yearned for this job. He could see himself standing up and collecting the arithmetic papers. He could see himself at Miss Patch's right hand while the class arose, row by row, to don their coats and hats. He could see himself opening the door the second before the bell rang, and admired how smartly he stood by the open door as the class filed out. When the class left, he knew just what he would have to do. He would erase the boards and sharpen the pencils on the teacher's desk, and take down yesterday's work from the walls and put up today's work. And when all this was done, it would be Pete Peters who locked the door behind the teacher and carried the key, like a courier, to the office keyboard.

Pete moved his eyes from the clock to Miss Patch. She was going to choose him, he knew.

Her glance flicked over the classroom. As if she were unaware that thirty pairs of eyes were fastened to her face — and that thirty tongues were being held expectantly still.

From her mouth came a low chuckle. She tucked her pencil behind her ear and folded her arms. "Goodness me," she said. "I wonder what I'm supposed to do now!"

The class answered as one. "Choose a helper!"

She smiled, a wide, amiable grin. Then her face grew solemn. She riffled through the papers on her desk. She stared ahead of her, looking carefully down each row. She pursed her lips and regarded the ceiling.

Pete felt his heart beating faster. He clasped his hands together so tightly that the knuckles showed white. "Please choose me," he wanted to shout. "Please choose me."

Miss Patch opened her mouth. "Will John Williams please stay after class?" she said offhandedly, as if the thing had been all decided long ago.

John bounced up, pink cheeked, and ready to take his place.

Pete pretended it didn't matter to him in the least. He made a great show of folding his arithmetic paper. He folded it in half, giving it his full attention. Next he folded the half in half again. He fitted the edges together carefully. He creased it firmly with his thumb, making the folded edge sharp. Then he turned slightly in his seat so that he could place it deep in his jeans pocket. Only then did he look up, casually, with unconcern, to see John Williams' broad, smiling face beaming out from beside the teacher's elbow.

It was a silly-looking face, Pete decided. "Teacher's pet," he flung out as he passed John on his way to the door. But John, if he heard, didn't so much as turn his head. Everyone knew there was nothing better than being a room helper.

5

PETE walked faster as he came within two blocks of home. Mish would be waiting. Good old Mish. Pete smiled thinking of his dog.

A woman opened her door and came out onto the porch. She looked carefully around and seeing him, called, "Young man!"

Pete looked around to see whom she was talking to and guessed it must be he.

"Did you call me?" he asked to make sure.

"Do you know who owns that big black dog?"

Pete looked at her; he hesitated. "What's the matter?" he asked carefully.

"A big black dog keeps walking into my house,"

she said fretfully. "If you happen to see the owners, will you tell them to keep the dog home?"

"Yes, I will," said Pete. "I certainly will."

He walked on quickly. He guessed Mish thought this house was their own house. All the houses on this block looked alike. He wasn't surprised that Mish got a little mixed up.

At the house on the corner a woman was just back-ending out of her car. It was a small sports car, shiny new, sitting close to the curb like a small pup. Pete stopped to examine it. The woman looked at him sharply, and he smiled.

"You aren't," she said, "by any chance, the boy who owns the big black dog, are you?"

Pete was careful. "What seems to be the matter?"

"Well, someone's big black hound jumped into my car this morning and wouldn't get out!" Her voice held sharp annoyance. "The car's not big enough for both of us. I missed my dentist appointment." She closed the door then and locked it.

"I guess he just wanted a ride," said Pete quickly.

"It seems to me," she said, "that the owner should teach his dog not to jump into other people's cars!"

"I'll tell him," he said, "if I see him," and walked on.

As he rounded the corner, he came upon a small corner garden so strange appearing that he stopped to examine it. It looked as if it was planted with weeds. Freshly planted. Some of the clumps were planted upside down.

Around the corner of the house came a woman in jeans and an old gardening jacket, with a trowel in her hand. She looked mad. She came down to the sidewalk garden.

"Someone keeps digging them back in," she said. "Every time I pull things out, someone lays them back in."

Pete blinked. "Who did you say?"

She looked at him sharply. "I didn't say!"

"It wasn't me!" he said stepping back.

"Well, it was somebody around here. Although who would keep doing a fool trick like that is more than I can figure." She started pulling the weeds out again. She turned to Pete again. "I suppose you wouldn't have any idea who it would be," she said suspiciously.

Pete scratched his head, thinking. "I can't think who it would be!" he said, and hurried on. He decided it couldn't be Mish. Anyway he was sure Mish was only trying to help. The more he thought about it, the prouder he was of Mish. Imagine a dog trying to *plant* things. Most dogs just dug them up. But then Mish, he had known all along, wasn't an ordinary dog.

Two women were chatting at the gate on the next corner. They looked at him curiously as he passed and resumed their conversation.

"Well, I'll tell you what I'd do, if a hound like that rang *my* doorbell! I'd call the police, that's what I'd do."

Pete hurried right by. He wondered if Mish really did ring that woman's doorbell. He was a little surprised that a dog could ring anybody's doorbell, but the more he thought about it, the less surprised he was. After all, Mish was an extraordinary dog. It made him proud of Mish. Real proud.

"Here Mish!" he called as he reached his own house. "Here Mish, old boy."

Mish came bounding around the house. He barked, and he yapped and he stood up on his hind legs. He made such a commotion that Mrs. Peters opened the back door.

"You glad to see me, old boy? You're pretty glad, huh. Well I'm just as glad to see you." Pete looked up. "Oh. Hi, Mom!"

Mrs. Peters held the door open until he and Mish came in. She didn't say Hi or Hello or anything like that. She said, "He howls. When he's tied up, he howls like a banshee."

Pete picked up the glass of milk his mother placed on the table for him and drank it down. Mrs. Peters sighed and Pete pretended not to hear the sound. He sat there and watched his mother put away the groceries. Buttermilk biscuits, pancake and waffle flour, quick-mix date bars, nothing-to-add-but-water angel food cake.

"Angel food cake?" said Pete.

"I bought a quick fudge mix, too," his mother said. "I thought maybe you and perhaps the little girl next door might get together and make some for yourselves."

Pete grunted. He and his old pal Tom used to make fudge on the front burner. "I think I'd like to try something different this time," he said casually, picking up the box of angel food cake.

Mrs. Peters turned around in surprise. She shrugged. "If you can make quick-mix fudge — you can certainly manage quick-mix angel food cake."

She finished putting all the other packages away, and put on her hat. "I have an appointment at the hairdressers," she explained. "I'll be back in time for dinner." She called back over her shoulder, "Be sure to clean up after yourself!"

She opened the door, and then looked back in

at Mish. "You'd better keep Mish right with you," she said, with a worry wrinkle on her face. "Right here with you all the time," she advised.

Pete turned the box to read the directions. "Sure," he said. "Come here, Mish," he called.

Mish obligingly came there. Pete seated himself on the kitchen stool. "Sit down, Mish," he invited.

Mish sat down, too. He placed his back end on a kitchen chair and his front feet on the floor. One of his back legs was curled under him. He grinned at Pete. Pete opened the box.

"It's just as easy as fudge," Pete said happily to Mish a few minutes later. Pete licked the spoon while Mish took the bowl. Mish grinned happily. They sat there companionably while the cake baked.

Pete opened the oven door and looked in. "It's baking all right," he reported. Mish came over to see for himself, and Pete obligingly held the door open so he could see.

"What I'm going to do," Pete explained to

Mish, "is just bring this cake, kind of offhand. And I'll say — " Pete frowned. He couldn't think of a thing to say that would explain a whole cake. "I guess maybe I'll bring her a big slice," he decided. "I'll take *two* slices to her; one for her to eat there and one to take home."

Pete cleaned up the kitchen and set the dishwasher going. He looked proudly around; he hadn't made much of a mess at all. His mother would be pleased.

"Here Mish," he called. He remembered that Mish had ducked out when the dishwasher went on. Pete looked into the other room. "Mish?" he called. The oven timer rang then, and Pete took the cake out, hurriedly, and turned it upside down on the wire rack, the way the directions said, before going to look for Mish. He couldn't help thinking how pleased Miss Patch would be when she saw the cake.

"Here, Mish!" he called. He looked in his bedroom and the other bedroom, too. He walked through the living room and back into the kitchen. He listened. He heard Mish yapping, then the sound of a man's voice hollering. Pete dashed to the front door.

The postman sat on the top step, his arm stiffly outstretched and in his shaking fingers a letter. Around his wrist Mish had playfully set his mouth. Mish's tail wagged, but his mouth was set firm.

"He just wants you to let him carry the letter," Pete tried to explain. "If you'll just let him help you carry it — " Pete grasped Mish's collar as he talked and pulled him away. The letter drifted to the ground, and Mish dashed at it. He picked it up and carried it proudly into the house.

The mailman examined his hand carefully.

"See," said Pete with a smile, "he wasn't going to bite you. He just wanted to help. He was only friendly!"

The mailman stood up. He lowered his head and glared into Pete's happy face. "As a mail carrier, I am a representative of the United States

Government. And speaking for the United States Government — I don't need any help! You get me?"

Pete nodded, went into the house and closed the door. He was sure the President of the United States wouldn't blame Mish for just trying to help.

Pete turned the cake out of the pan and set it right side up. He looked at it. Then he took the cake box out of the garbage can and regarded the picture of the angel food cake on it.

"They must have put in the wrong mix," Pete said. For his angel food cake was no higher than a one-layer. That's all it was — just a flat, ordinary cake. Mish looked at it, too.

"I guess you can have it, Mish," said Pete, feeling mad at the company for making such a mistake.

Mish sniffed at it, and backed away. Pete picked it up and carried it outside and gently laid it on top of the refuse in the garbage can. He decided he'd think of something else to give to the teacher.

"I met most of the people in the neighborhood today," said Mrs. Peters as she took her place at the dinner table. There was an odd quality to her voice. Both Pete and Mr. Peters glanced at her.

"Practically everybody," she said.

Mr. Peters helped himself to the cooked vegetables. "That must have been pleasant," he said.

Pete didn't say anything. He had a strange feeling that what his mother was going to say next was not what his father expected to hear.

"Mrs. Anderson called, for one," she said.

Mr. Peters put some more butter on his bread. "Who is Mrs. Anderson?"

"She lives across the street," said Mrs. Peters.

"Well, isn't that nice of her to call," said Mr. Peters.

"Very," said Mrs. Peters dryly. "She called to inform me that although she has nothing against dogs in general, she feels that any dog who opens the door and walks in uninvited is more than she can appreciate."

"You mean Mish did that?" said Mr. Peters. Pete was not at all surprised.

"Mrs. Anderson told me over the telephone that ordinarily she would have called the police, but under the circumstances, seeing we were new in the neighborhood, she thought it would be more friendly to call us."

"That *was* nice of her," said Mr. Peters.

"You can't blame a dog for being friendly!" said Pete.

"And then Mrs. Chapley called."

Mr. Peters stopped eating. "You don't mean to say Mish was visiting there, too?"

"Oh no," said Mrs. Peters. "He was much more helpful there. He *helped* her clean the garage. After she had piled everything up for the Salvation Army truck, Mish dragged everything across the yard and into the street."

Mr. Peters pursed his lips.

Pete said quickly, "You can't blame a dog for wanting to help."

"Of course not!" said Mr. Peters heartily.

"I can!" said Mrs. Peters. She arose and went into the kitchen and turned on the coffee.

Mr. Peters regarded the food on his plate thoughtfully.

"A Mrs. Johnson dropped in," said Mrs. Peters reseating herself.

"Complaint?" asked Mr. Peters.

"Not exactly. She just was curious to know who were the owners of the big black friendly dog!"

"That's all?"

Mrs. Peters nodded. "She said she just wanted to know, that's all."

"Oh," said Mr. Peters.

"That's what I thought," said Pete's mother.

There was a silence. "Well," said Mr. Peters, "I hope that's all."

"That's all I *know* about," said Mrs. Peters. Pete looked down at his plate.

The telephone rang. Mrs. Peters answered it. "Why yes," she said, and glanced quickly at Mr. Peters. Mr. Peters stopped eating. Pete stopped eating, too.

Mrs. Peters listened. She frowned. She listened some more. Pete fidgeted. "Thank you," said Mrs. Peters politely. "Thank you for telling us — first," she added. She hung up, came back and sat down at the table.

"Something important?" said Mr. Peters helping himself to more potatoes.

"Well, that depends on whether you like milk," said Mrs. Peters. "That was the milk company."

"The milk company? Didn't they get their check?"

"Oh, they got their check all right. What's doubtful is whether we are going to get their milk. They just wanted to tell us that their drivers are quite capable of delivering milk without any outside help. If it's all the same with us, that is."

"Can't you see," said Pete beginning to feel desperate, "Mish was probably just being friendly."

Mr. Peters had stopped eating. He pursed his lips and looked quickly at his wife and then at his son. He looked long and earnestly at his son.

"Hmmm," he said then, and drank his coffee.

6

BEFORE Pete opened his eyes the next morning, he had a strange feeling that his head was resting on a rock. He wriggled his shoulders, and at the firmness below them, he opened his eyes. Pete sat up. He was not in his bed at all. He was on the floor. Pete put one hand on the bed and raised himself up. Sleeping in his bed was Mish — Mish with his head on Pete's pillow and the covers snugly drawn up over his shoulders.

"Mish!" shouted Pete, and yanked the covers off. Mish opened one eye, and wagged his tail, grinning joyously.

"Good gravy, Mish," said Pete. "You didn't

have to go and push me out of bed."

Mish sat up. He didn't seem to be at all abashed.

"I guess you had a bed to yourself before; I guess that's it," Pete said. He frowned, looking around the room. He was pretty sure his mother wouldn't let him have another bed in his room — just for Mish. Pete sighed.

"Down Mish!" he said firmly. "Down!" He pointed to the floor.

Mish looked down at the braided rug at the bedside, then yawned noisily. With that he lay down on the bed again and closed his eyes. Pete stood there, gazing at him thoughtfully. Mish opened one eye and looked at Pete, then he wriggled, nesting his paws up under his chin. Pete pulled the covers up over him and closed the bedroom door quietly.

His mother yawned as she poured his glass of milk. "I don't know what's the matter with me lately," she remarked. "I can't seem to keep my eyes open."

Pete yawned too. He knew what was the matter

with him, but he didn't say anything.

"Well, I know what's the matter with me!" stated Mr. Peters. He yawned too. "You know I got up three times last night to let that dog out." He looked sternly at Pete.

"I guess it was because he was brought up in a hotel."

"If you ask me," said Mrs. Peters, "that dog wasn't brought up at all. Someone just opened the door and there he was." She shivered.

Mr. Peters laughed. "You talk as if poor Mish were a monster."

"I can't think of a better description," she said.

Pete ate his cereal methodically, pointedly ignoring both his parents.

Anybody would be lucky to have a dog like Mish, he thought.

After breakfast he went down into the basement and looked around. He didn't see another bed there. He didn't see even a mattress, but he did stumble over the old sleeping bag his father had bought him when Pete was a cub scout. Pete picked it up. He wondered how Mish would like sleeping in a sleeping bag. He carried it upstairs and into his bedroom. Mish was still asleep, so he stuck it into the closet, and closed the door softly behind him again. Pete smiled; he rubbed the back of his shoulders. It would be good sleeping in his own bed tonight.

Pete went on outside and looked around. Back in his old home there was plenty doing on Saturday morning; but there was nothing much doing here at all. Pete sighed. He wished Mish would wake up. The screen door on the house next door banged and Wanda Sparling came out. She put a brass instrument to her mouth and blew. A high sour note came out. Pete showed his pain on his face.

"I'm taking trumpet lessons," she announced, and brought the instrument up to her mouth again.

Pete clapped his hands over his ears. "It sounds to me like a good idea," he said. "When do you start?"

Wanda stuck her nose in the air. "I've been

taking trumpet lessons for a year!" she said haughtily. And placed the instrument to her lips again.

"Hah!" said Pete. "Well, you'd better not practice that around Mish," he said warningly. "Dogs have very sensitive ears. Some dogs even go mad when they hear some sounds — like trumpets," he added.

Wanda frowned. She lowered the trumpet. "Personally," she said, "if I were you, I wouldn't worry about Mish going mad — from what I hear around here — it's much more likely the whole neighborhood will go mad! Do you know that my mom keeps the door locked now — all the time!"

Pete looked quickly over his shoulder. He hoped Wanda's voice hadn't carried to his mother.

"Ahh," said Pete, "he wouldn't hurt anything. He's just friendly."

Wanda sniffed. "He's too friendly, if you ask me."

"Well, I'm not asking you," retorted Pete, and

66

went back into his own house. Mish came slithering down the steps from upstairs at the sound of Pete's voice, emitting little excited yelps, and jumped on him and licked his face and his eyes and his hair. Pete had difficulty staying on his feet. But he hugged Mish extra hard. After all, Mish was a pretty good dog.

"Good dog," he said to Mish now, rubbing his coat, "good dog, good dog." Mish wagged his tail, and yelped and rolled over in ecstasy.

"Good grief!" came Pete's mother's voice from upstairs. "What's all that racket about?"

"It's just me!" called Pete.

His mother came down the stairs; her full cotton skirt swirled around as she moved. "Mrs. Barnes and Mrs. Engstrom are coming for coffee," she said. Mrs. Peters looked at Mish and frowned slightly. Mish grinned back at her and she took a step backward quickly.

"Why don't you and Mish take a walk?" she asked brightly. "After all, he is so playful," she said in that same purposefully bright tone. "I really don't think Mrs. Engstrom would understand Mish's — " she hesitated; "exuberance," she said, pleased with the word.

Pete looked at his mother. He could always tell when she was trying not to hurt his feelings. Unlike his father, she would use long words that softened the harshness of the meaning. His father was not handicapped by any such nicety. He

guessed his mother didn't want Mish around while she was having company.

"Don't you worry about Mish," he promised. "I'll take care of him." He grasped Mish firmly by the collar and led him into the kitchen. But Mish wasn't very much interested in breakfast; he was more interested in the doorbell ringing. And at the sound of the ladies' voices, he bounded out.

"Mish!" shouted Pete. Pete ran into the living room. Mish was not there, but Pete looked around quickly and smiled politely.

"Mrs. Engstrom, this is my son, Pete," said Mrs. Peters.

"How do you do," said Pete politely. Mish came sliding in and Pete grabbed hold of his collar. Mish smiled — a big brash friendly smile with his tongue lolling out and his eyes gleaming.

"And this is his dog, Mish," said Mrs. Peters hastily.

Mish surged forward but was held back by Pete's hold on him. Mrs. Engstrom stepped back.

"Nice doggie," she said uncertainly.

Mrs. Peters went on with the introductions. "And this is Mrs. — " She paused and looked around. "I guess Mrs. Barnes is still hanging up her coat in the entry hall. But she walked quickly back to the front entrance. With a sudden feeling of dread, Pete followed.

"Mrs. Barnes?" called Mrs. Peters lightly. "May I help — oh!" Mrs. Barnes was not there. The closet door was closed. Suddenly a knocking was heard.

"Mrs. Barnes!" shouted Mrs. Peters, and rushed to the closet. She opened it. Blinking, Mrs. Barnes stood there crushed against the coats.

"My goodness," she said. "The strangest thing. Someone pushed the door closed." She looked around at the assembled women and wonderingly her glance fell on Pete.

"I wasn't even here," said Pete quickly. He didn't look at Mish. Mrs. Barnes' gaze went from Pete to Mish. Mish grinned and took a step forward.

"He's just playful," said Pete quickly, pulling back on Mish's collar.

"Well, he certainly is!" she said and walking warily past him, she followed the other ladies into the living room.

7

"COME ON, Mish," said Pete, and grasping him firmly, he led him out the back door. He stood on the back step and looked around the yard. He picked up a stick and tossed it. "Go get it, Mish," he said. Mish cocked one eye toward the spot where the stick had landed. Then he turned around and batted lightly at the kitchen door.

"You can't go in there, Mish," said Pete. He picked up another stick and tossed it again. "Come on, boy," he said, "go get it."

Mish didn't even turn his head. He stood up on his hind legs and placed his paw on the doorknob.

"Oh, for heaven's sake, Mish," said Pete. He

picked Mish up and half carried, half dragged him to the middle of the yard. "Mom doesn't want us in there, can't you see that?" In spite of himself there was a bit of resentment in his voice. And hearing it, he put his arms around Mish and hugged him hard, pressing his face against Mish's body. "I guess we can go in there if we really want to," he said. He looked around. "Of course, there's no reason why we shouldn't stay out here a while, either."

But Mish didn't seem to agree with him. Mish, as soon as Pete let go of him, started back toward the kitchen door.

"Mish!" shouted Pete. "You come back here!" But Mish paid no attention. Pete sighed. He followed Mish to the back door. Pete looked in the small window. No one was in the kitchen. He put his hand on Mish's collar and stealthily he opened the door. Making as little noise as possible, he tiptoed through the kitchen, ducked around the open doorway and sneaked upstairs into his bedroom and closed the door behind himself and Mish.

"Okay, fella, relax," he said. Pete flopped down on his bed. Mish jumped up on the bed, too; and Pete got up, went to the closet, rolled out his sleeping bag, and placed Mish on it. "There you are, fella," he said, "it's all yours." Pete stretched out comfortably on his own bed.

Mish jumped lightly from the sleeping bag to the bed. He lay down between Pete and the wall so that Pete had to roll aside to make room for Mish's head on the pillow. It was pretty crowded that way. Pete sat up. He slid off the bed and looked from Mish to the sleeping bag. Then Pete lay down on the sleeping bag. Settling himself as comfortably as he could, he rested his hands behind his head, and stared up at the ceiling.

He gave some thought to Mish. "Good dog," he said automatically.

The bed shook above him as Mish tried to wag his tail under the coverlet. Mish really was a good dog, Pete reflected, as playful and friendly as you'd ever want a dog to be. Wanda had said he was *too friendly*. Pete frowned. He let his thoughts dwell on Wanda. She thought she was so smart to bring a present to the teacher. He wished he had a present to bring to Miss Patch — something unusual and wonderful — something that would make her eyebrows go up and her teeth stick out in a smile.

Pete wriggled his shoulders. He saw himself lugging this great big box into the schoolroom. "What is it?" everyone would ask. "Whatever is it?" He saw with satisfaction that Wanda Sparling's eyes *bugged* out. Miss Patch came in. She stopped, still. She clapped her hands. "Why, it's a present!" she said, with surprise in her voice — "A present for me!" Pete smiled, with his eyes closed. In his mind he saw Wanda Sparling, her dark eyes flashing, her lips pursed. Pete turned over on his side. He heard a tinkling of laughter from downstairs.

"Quiet, Mish," he said as Mish jumped off the bed and went to the bedroom door. Mish listened a moment. Then he turned around and jumped back up on the bed. But he sat up now and then when the laughter from the living room reached his ears.

Pete didn't know when he fell asleep. But asleep he must have been, for suddenly he was back at school and it was three o'clock. Miss Patch was about to name the room helper. Pete felt the tension within him. His hands held tightly together, he gazed at the teacher, hoping, by his gaze to impel her to say his name. But Miss Patch looked right over his head. She spoke out the name of the boy who sat directly behind Pete — and then she called the name of the girl behind him.

Up and down the rows she went, naming every boy and girl, loud and clear — everyone, that is, but Pete. Pete crouched in his seat behind his arithmetic book, his ears burning. He could hear Wanda Sparling, hollering above everyone else. He moved his head. The shriek had seemed startlingly close.

Pete opened his eyes. Then he sprang up. The shriek was close, all right. It had come from downstairs and carried right through the open doorway into his bedroom.

Pete dashed downstairs. Mrs. Barnes, Mrs. Engstrom and his mother were sitting at the table — and so was Mish. Mrs. Engstrom still had her mouth open.

"Mish!" yelled Pete. But Mish merely set one paw on the table, calmly helped himself to Mrs. Barnes' slice of cake and looked over at Mrs. Peters as if he were waiting for a cup of coffee.

"Come on, Mish," Pete coaxed as he grabbed his collar. "Come on, boy." Mish resisted.

Mrs. Engstrom moved her chair as far back from the table as she could get. Mrs. Barnes' face turned red with indignation. "That's *my* cake!" she said to the dog.

Mish obligingly turned his head and put his nose into Mrs. Engstrom's dish.

"Out! Nuisance!" shouted Mrs. Engstrom. She picked up her handbag and brought it smartly down on Mish's head. "Shoo!" she said.

The grin slid off Mish's face. He looked about bewildered. "He wasn't trying to hurt you!" shouted Pete. "He was just trying to be friendly!" He pulled Mish off the chair and dragged him toward the kitchen.

"Pete!"

Pete had never heard his mother's voice sound quite like this before. He stopped. It looked almost as if his mother was going to cry. Pete quickly glanced away. His eyes rested on the table. The pretty blue cloth was stained with spilled coffee, the half-eaten slices of cake lay on the wet spot. A cup was overturned on its saucer. And the two ladies sat there looking disapproving. Everybody his mother had met since they moved into this new house had been unfriendly. And it was all because of Mish.

Pete knew what he had to do. He guessed he had known from the first moment he had awakened this morning. He took a firmer hold of Mish's collar. "C'mon, Mish," he said. He dragged Mish through the kitchen to the back door. Mish sat back on his haunches. Pete tried to keep his voice steady. "You gotta come, Mish."

Mish grinned at him, and Pete dropped to his knees and pressed his face against Mish's coat. Mish quivered with affection. "I can't help it, Mish," Pete whispered. "I just can't help it. You've got to go back, don't you see. You've got to!"

Pete pressed his face against Mish until he could talk again. "It isn't your fault, Mish. It's them! They don't understand you. What you need is someone who appreciates a dog like you."

Mish yawned. He looked longingly toward the bedroom.

"Don't you see, Mish —" said Pete, holding him back, "this is just not the right home for you!" The last words stuck in his throat. But he swallowed hard.

8

PETE closed the kitchen door softly behind him. "Come on, Mish," he said. "Come on."

He crossed the street with Mish at his heels. He pretended they were just going for a walk. Pete puckered his lips but the sounds that came out were totally unlike a whistle. He ran his tongue around his lips. He passed the school, but he didn't see it. He went up Cherry Street and down Pine.

He talked bravely to Mish all the way there. "The old man will be glad to see you!" he said. "I bet he missed you!" He looked at Mish trotting along happily. "I'm going to miss you," he said. "I'll come to see you," he offered. "I'll come to see you often. Maybe every day after school. I won't ever let them get me another dog. Because — no other dog in the world could be like you."

Pete smiled wryly at his own words. Funny — that's exactly what his mother had said.

He came to the gas station. A man was working on a car with his head under the hood. He wore old army trousers and a greasy shirt. Pete's feet dragged. He skirted the empty lot. The roof of the shack had fallen in. This surprised him and he stopped for a minute, looking at the shell that remained. He felt as if a long, long time had elapsed since he had been here last. Long enough for a little shack like this one to crumble and, finally, for the roof to fall in. Then he went on, walking a little hurriedly past the house with the boarded-up windows. He didn't like houses that were closed and still. He didn't like houses without people in them. He hurried past.

But a new fear filled him as he reached the little white fence. Mish sniffed at the ground around him.

"C'mon, Mish," said Pete, softly. "C'mon, boy."

He turned up the narrow brick walk lined with flowers and raised his eyes to the little red house — and then he stopped.

There was no little house there!

Pete looked around him. There was the white fence, the brick path, the flowers — but that was all.

Pete rubbed his eyes. His scalp prickled; he took a step backward. Then he turned around. He ran down the brick walk, out of the little yard surrounded by a white fence. With Mish at his heels, he streaked past the boarded-up house, past the tumbled-down shack, and breathlessly charged into the gas station.

The man behind the hood raised his head. Pete pointed and gulped a breath of air.

"Eh?" said the man, and put one grimy hand to his ear as if Pete had said something he had missed.

Pete gulped air again. And Mish sat back on his haunches, panting after the dash.

The man looked at Pete. "Well, for heaven's

sake," said the man, "you back again?"

Pete exhaled slowly. "What happened to him?" he asked.

The mechanic looked from Mish to Pete. Then back to Mish again. "He looks all right to me," he said.

Mish yawned.

"I mean the man in the little red house down the street," said Pete.

The man looked vaguely down the street. He scratched his head.

"People in trailers just come and go," he said. He seemed to like the sound of it. "They just come and go. Here today, gone tomorrow." He shrugged. "I guess I'm funny that way," he said. "I like to stay put."

Pete placed his teeth over his lower lip to keep it from trembling. The man took a rag from his pocket and wiped his fingers.

"Now you take this street," he said. "People moving in and out. That's the way it's always been. But the next street over. Why, some peo-

ple have been living there for years. Would you believe it?" he said as if he was hard put to believe it himself. "That church has been there for twenty-five years."

Pete looked in the direction of the man's out-stretched finger. Over the trees he could see the steeple of the church. A wooden steeple.

"Never turned chick nor child away from his door. That's what they say of him," said the mechanic. The man leaned closer and whispered. "They say he himself was left in a basket at a church door when he was a baby and that's why he turned preacher." The mechanic nodded.

Pete blinked. "You wouldn't by any chance," he said with new hope, "happen to know where the man in the little red house went?"

The mechanic stuck his head under the hood again. "Nope," he said. "I never ask them where they go. When they leave, I say good riddance. That's what I say."

Pete sighed. He looked around then at the old garage, the dirty mechanic and Mish, who had curled up at his feet and fallen asleep. "You wouldn't by any chance want — "

The man raised his head and grinned at him. "That's one thing we got plenty of around here," he said, "and that's dogs!"

"C'mon, Mish," said Pete.

Pete walked down the street. He came to a white house with pink shutters and a well-cared-for little lawn. He stopped at the gate, looking at the neat flower beds and the polished doorknob. Then he shook his head and walked onward. The next house looked more promising, he thought. It needed paint, there was a doll buggy, turned upside down on the walk. A big hole was in the middle of the front yard and a broken swing hung from the bough of a cherry tree. As he stood there looking about him a woman opened the door. She threw a suspicious glance at him. Then she turned her head back into the house. "Virgil!" Her voice was shrill. "You clean up your room, do you hear me! And don't you leave tracks when you walk through my clean kitchen."

Pete walked on. He didn't even pause at the next two houses. Mish was a special kind of dog and needed a special kind of home. Mish needed a home where he wasn't just a dog. He needed someone who could appreciate him. Pete walked on and on. Whenever he saw somebody working on a lawn he'd say — "Say, would you like a dog? He's an awfully friendly dog."

One man said, "If he's such a good dog, why are you trying to get rid of him?"

Another said, "You'd better take that dog right back where you got him, sonny" — and, "You won't get a thing for him anyway."

One woman just slammed the door in his face. "Get that hound off my property," is what she said.

Pete walked on, telling himself that he would soon find a home for Mish. Somebody pretty soon now would take a look at good old Mish, and want him for his dog.

9

WANDA SPARLING came out of her house and watched as Pete came slowly down his own street with Mish still at his side. Seeing her, an idea came to Pete.

"Hi, Wanda," he called.

"Hi," she answered cautiously.

He came toward her pulling the dog. "I've been thinking, Wanda," he said.

She looked at him with suspicion. "That must have been hard."

He ignored this thrust. "There's good old Wanda Sparling, I've been thinking. With nothing to do but practice her trumpet and no one to play with."

"But you," she put in cuttingly.

"That's right," he nodded. "But me —" he paused — "and my dog. I've been thinking — old Mish here is just crazy about you!"

Wanda patted Mish's nose and he repaid her with wet kisses.

"See?" Pete said.

Wanda wiped her face. "See what?" she said.

"I'm going to give this dog to you!"

Wanda stood up. "Oh no you're not, Pete Peters. My mother wouldn't let me have a dog like this. She says he's not a dog — he's a character. She says — next time he tries to help her take the clothes off the line, she's going to call the humane society. She says it's all right with her to have friendly neighbors, but she draws the line at friendly dogs. She says —"

"All right, all right," said Pete crossly. "I get the picture. You don't want Mish."

"I don't want Mish," said Wanda, "period."

Pete sank down and put his arms around Mish. Wanda companionably sat herself down beside him. She patted Mish's shiny black coat. "He's gotta go, huh?" she said.

Pete nodded. All at once he couldn't trust himself to speak.

"I do like him!" said Wanda. She threw her arms around Mish and gave him a hug.

Pete sat up. "Then you will ask your mother — "

Wanda loosened her hold. "No," she said, and Pete sighed.

"You could take him to the animal shelter," said Wanda helpfully. "When our old cat had kittens and nobody wanted them, we just took them to the animal shelter and — " She paused.

"And what?" said Pete.

Wanda shook her head. "I guess the animal shelter is no place for a friendly dog like Mish."

"There must be somebody in this world who wants a nice friendly dog like Mish," said Pete.

"Who?"

Pete couldn't think who. "What we've got to do," he thought aloud, "is find somebody who lives alone."

Wanda looked at him with scorn. "Just because you live alone is no sign you're lonely. Besides the only one I know who lives alone around here is Mr. Harvey. But he's a birdwatcher."

Pete felt his scalp tingle. "You mean he's balmy?"

"A birdwatcher," Wanda explained with unnecessary emphasis, "is a person who watches birds. Mr. Harvey keeps records of which birds live here in the winter, and which fly away — and all that."

"Hah!" said Pete. "Old Mish here would be a lot more interesting to watch than a bunch of birds. Why I bet Mr. Harvey could write a whole book about Mish!" Pete stood up. "Maybe even a whole roomful of books — " He caught Wanda's pitying glance and sat down again.

"Well, who else you got in mind?"

Wanda pursed her lips. She looked far off into the distance. Pete looked too. A white wooden steeple made a sharp point over the rooftops.

"If he was a horse," offered Wanda, "we could just turn him out to pasture — somewhere."

"Ever see a horse who wanted to sit down and eat with people?"

"I never saw a *dog* like Mish before."

Pete looked at Wanda. "There never was a dog like Mish before," Pete said and suddenly there was a large lump in his throat.

"Reverend Mulby says," said Wanda, "that every animal can teach us something. Like modesty from cats, and honest toil from ants — "

"Who said that?" said Pete looking out toward the white steeple.

"Reverend Mulby."

"Is he the one that never turns 'chick nor child' from his door?"

"How could he?" said Wanda philosophically, "when he himself was found in a — "

"Basket!" They breathed the word together and looked at each other with growing excitement.

"Do you think — " began Pete, coming to his feet.

"The first thing we have to do," said Wanda standing up too, "is find a basket."

Pete looked at Mish. He felt a little troubled without knowing exactly why. "I think it would be better if we asked him first."

Wanda said, "Nobody's going to take Mish if you *ask* them first."

"It doesn't seem fair to Mish to just dump him on a doorstep," Pete said.

"Personally," said Wanda, "I think it's not fair to Rev — "

"Okay," said Pete quickly. "We'll find a basket."

They couldn't find a basket big enough, but they did find a large, empty carton in the alley behind the church. Pete lifted Mish and put him in, trying it for size. Mish yawned and settled down in the bottom of the box.

Wanda found a piece of string — a broken kite tail tangled with it. Pete pulled the string off,

closed the top of the carton, leaving a wide slit
for air, and tied the top down after a fashion. Then
he took his new ball-point pen out of his pocket

and looked around for something to write on. He looked through his pockets but could find nothing but an old carefully folded arithmetic paper. He looked at it. A large 100 was scrawled on the upper third of the page in red pencil. It ran right over his name — Pete Peters, Fifth Grade — and almost covered it. Satisfied, Pete turned the paper over, and using the box as a writing place, he printed carefully: "Please take care of Mish and he will love you forever."

Then quickly he refolded the paper, and put it under the knotted string at the top of the box.

There was no bell on the church door, so they just banged on the door a couple of times and turned and ran. They ran down the steps, vaulted the box hedge and crouched low behind the thick lilac clump at the corner. Here they could see the church door and the box.

Wanda's elbow sharply dug into his side. "Remember it was *my* idea," she said, sounding pleased with herself.

Pete moved away a bit. He was sure he would have thought of it himself anyway.

Pete waited anxiously, keeping an eye on the bulging sides of the box. He wished the Reverend Mulby would come out quickly, for the sides of the box were beginning to shake precariously. He held his breath when he saw the door open, his head raised above the hedge, watching, waiting. Then he fell on his knees and ducked his head, pulling Wanda down too. For the person who came out of the Church door first was not Reverend Mulby — it was Miss Patch!

"Oh, my!" she said, loud and clear, for she almost stumbled over it.

Reverend Mulby came just behind her. "What is this?" he said.

Pete raised his head cautiously. Reverend Mulby had pulled the arithmetic paper open and was looking at it in puzzlement.

"Well, for goodness sake," said Miss Patch, "that looks as if it is — " She looked over the Reverend's shoulder. "Why that is Pete Peters' arithmetic paper!" she said in surprise. "I'd know it anywhere!" She turned it over and read the note on the other side.

"Peters?" said the preacher doubtfully.

"He's in my fifth grade," said Miss Patch. "He's a new boy and rather shy," she added.

Pete, behind the hedge, blushed, while Wanda put her fingers up to her mouth and giggled through them.

"A dog!" shouted Reverend Mulby, as Mish broke the string. "Why ever did the boy put a dog in the box?"

Pete scrunched even lower behind the hedge. He said between his clenched teeth — "It was your idea, remember." Wanda sniffed.

Miss Patch chuckled. "I guess it was supposed to be a present — a present for you."

"For me!" said Reverend Mulby. "Whatever would I do with a dog?"

"I wonder" — said Miss Patch — "whether Pete saw me stop here. I just wonder, now, if he

98

could have meant this as a present — for me!" She laughed, and Pete guessed that Mish was licking her face with his tongue. "My he's a friendly dog," she said.

Pete shuddered.

"I am sure he meant the dog as a present for you," Reverend Mulby said in a very firm voice.

Pete didn't wait to hear anything more. He turned and ran. He ran up the block and past the school, and all the way home. His feet pounded on the pavement and his heart pounded under his shirt.

He tore into the house and up the steps and into his bedroom — and he fell full length on his bed, screwed his eyes tight shut and pressed his face in his pillow. He thought of Miss Patch thinking Mish was a present from him — and he turned his face to the wall and wept.

10

THEY SPOKE softly to Pete at breakfast the next morning, as if someone in the house were sick. They talked to each other over his head with their eyes, and his father gave him a brand-new dime that he had just found in the bottom of his pocket.

"Thank you," Pete said politely, putting it in his pocket. He ate his oatmeal stolidly. He ate slowly, making breakfast time last as long as possible. No one mentioned Mish at all.

They thought he had taken Mish back to the man who had owned him. Pete hadn't told them the whole story. They thought he was worrying about Mish, missing him. But it wasn't Mish he was worried about, it was Miss Patch.

They talked about a dog, a puppy who could be trained to sleep in the basement and not jump on the table. But Pete didn't listen very carefully. He wasn't interested in a puppy at that moment.

"The best thing for you to do is get yourself right off to school," said his mother in a purposefully bright tone.

Pete looked at her blankly. The thing for him to do, he had already figured, was to stay as far away from school as he possibly could. He considered the possibility of shipping as cabin boy on a boat to Alaska.

". . . You'd better wear your slicker," his mother was saying.

Pete blinked, looking at his mother with surprise. Now how did she know what he was thinking!

"It's beginning to rain," she said, looking out the kitchen window.

Pete looked out the window, too. He shivered. It seemed suddenly to him terribly cold and wet.

Much too cold and wet for anyone to be going out, even to school.

"My goodness," said his mother, "it's raining cats and dogs!" Then she started, and looked guilty. His father cleared his throat warningly.

Pete sighed. He guessed he'd have to go to school after all. He allowed himself to be bundled into his yellow slicker and rain hat.

He sloshed through the mud puddles on his way to school. He kept his head low, suddenly glad for the rain hat that almost covered his face. By going through every puddle twice, he figured he'd get there just as the bell rang. He wasn't going to chance any encounter with Miss Patch before school began!

But he miscalculated; the bell had not yet rung when he reached school. And he stood on the wet playground wishing he were someplace else. Out of the corner of his eye he saw Miss Patch come to the front door and look around, but he flattened himself against the wall and pulled his hat down over his face.

Wanda slowly sloshed across the playground and came to stand next to him.

"We could tell her we've never seen Mish before," she suggested.

Under the circumstances, Pete appreciated the "we." His words to Wanda were kinder, he thought, than the suggestion deserved.

"Nah!" he said. "We couldn't do that."

"She said she *liked* dogs," said Wanda brightly.

"She won't like *this* dog," said Pete darkly. "Ladies don't seem to like Mish at all." Pete had to swallow.

"Funny," said Wanda reflectively, "I never really thought of teacher being a 'lady.' She's much nicer than most ladies."

Pete nodded. "That's because she doesn't pretend things are so when they aren't," he offered wisely.

Wanda gave him a quick look.

"Oh most ladies can't help it," said Pete. "That's just the way they are."

"Well most ladies like *most* friendly dogs," said

Wanda with her nose in the air.

"Huh," said Pete. "That's the trouble with Mish — he's *too* friendly."

They stood there, side by side, in the rain, waiting for the bell to ring.

"When I was in the third grade," said Wanda, "a boy brought a live snake to class and put it in the teacher's drawer."

"What did she do to him?" asked Pete anxiously.

Wanda glanced quickly at Pete. "Look Pete," she said, "whatever they do to you they'll have to do to me too. I'll tell them it was really my idea. That's what I'll tell them." Pete eyed Wanda carefully. She seemed to be pleased with the picture of herself standing up in front of the teacher bravely taking all the blame on herself. She seemed to be much too pleased.

"No," said Pete. "It was my dog. You'd better stay out of it."

"I'm in it!" said Wanda. "I'm in it with you."

"I don't want you in it!" said Pete, wishing she had stayed out of it in the first place. "You get me,

I don't want you in it at all!" He stuck his face close to hers and glowered.

Wanda set her lip stubbornly and marched ahead of him into the room.

Pete slid into his seat and slumped low, avoiding Miss Patch's eye. But by not so much as a word nor a glance did she single him out that morning. She seemed unusually preoccupied. And not only Pete, but the whole class felt it. He could tell by the shuffling of feet up and down the row, and the innumerable trips to the water fountain. Out of the corner of his eye he could see John Williams chewing gum but Miss Patch appeared not to notice it. She spent most of their study period with her chin in her hands, staring out of the window at the kindergarten room. Once she sighed. And the whole class seemed to sigh with her.

Startled, she looked around. For the first time that day she seemed to really look at the class — for the first time she smiled.

Pete lowered his head and stared hard at his social studies book. He avoided looking at her so she would not look at him. When he broke his pencil point, he chewed it back to a point industriously, behind the lid of his desk, so that he would not have to arise and walk down the aisle and past the teacher's desk to the pencil sharpener in the corner of the room. Cutting out colored pieces of paper for his notebook cover, he pushed the scraps into his pocket rather than get up and put them in the wastebasket beside the teacher's desk. When she asked the class at large a question, he raised his hand with the others — but he raised it gently, not too high, not waving it wildly around — and he breathed a sigh of relief as her eye passed over him and settled on the more extended arms about him. He walked a tightrope, so to speak, all afternoon, not leaning too far this way, nor too far that, placing one foot before the other carefully.

He held his breath every time Miss Patch raised her head. And he kept his head lowered, and whenever possible a book in front of it, hiding himself from her view.

When she asked for volunteers to hang the map

on the board, he raised his hand politely, but he didn't spring to her assistance as three other boys did. At recess he cautiously moved to the farthest end of the playfield. At gym he looked the other way when Miss Patch looked about for a partner. When the minute hand jumped to three, he could hardly hide his impatience to get out of the room, away from Miss Patch. He kept his eye on the clock, as if its slow pace fascinated him, his ears strained for the sound of the bell. He measured the

distance from his seat to the door, and shifted half out of his seat for a good start.

Miss Patch tapped three times with her pencil on the edge of the desk. She said softly, "It would give me great pleasure if you would stay and be my helper tonight —"

The bell rang. And he was already out of his seat before he heard the name from her lips.

" — Pete Peters," she said.

Pete turned away from the door. Reluctantly he went to stand by her elbow. The other day he had prayed that he be chosen. Today, by a wry turn of fate, his prayer had been answered.

The door closed on the last pupil, and he turned slowly, looking fearfully at Miss Patch.

She sat down at her desk and leaned way back in her chair that tipped.

And because his legs felt suddenly weak, Pete sat down, too.

"Do you know what Mish did last night?"

"What?" asked Pete hoarsely, but somehow he had a pretty good idea already.

"He slept on my bed — all night!"

Pete looked at Miss Patch in surprise. She sounded pleased.

"My brother Pete used to have a dog that slept on his bed," she confided. She rolled her mouth around in a smile. "Oh, my, I was jealous."

She chuckled. "This morning Mish scared the milkman out of his wits." She laughed heartily. "I've always wanted a friendly dog," she said with satisfaction.

"You mean you *like* him?" asked Pete.

She leaned forward across her desk. "Mish is just about the nicest present I have ever received!"

Pete straightened his shoulders and raised his head. "He's not the kind of dog you can give to just anybody," he said.

Miss Patch nodded in agreement. She looked around quickly as if someone might be around to overhear. Then she whispered, "You know, I don't think it has ever occurred to Mish that he is a dog."

Pete opened his eyes wide. "It hasn't?"

Miss Patch shook her head. "Mish," she said with satisfaction, "is just like my brother Pete's dog. He thinks he's people. Why he sat right down at the kitchen table with me for breakfast," she laughed. "Oh, my," she said. "I can still hear my sisters' squeals when my brother Pete's dog did that!"

Suddenly a great weight lifted from Pete's heart. "Some of my mother's friends are like that," he confided.

"Do you know what else he did?"

Pete held his tongue between his teeth. He was almost afraid to guess.

Miss Patch's face crinkled with amusement. "He closed the door on me."

"When you were in the closet," supplied Pete.

Miss Patch threw back her head and laughed. "Oh, dear!" she said, shaking with laughter. "Oh, my!"

Pete smiled weakly.

"I never expected to find a sense of humor in an animal! He's a rare one!" she said with admiration.

111

"You can say that again," said Pete with a sigh of relief. Miss Patch liked Mish. She *liked* it when he opened and shut doors. She *liked* his sitting at the table and eating breakfast with her. She even liked his sleeping on her bed.

"I'm going to get him a bed of his own," said Miss Patch with a smile.

Pete wondered if Miss Patch had awakened this morning sleeping on the floor. He didn't ask her.

"Mish likes to plant things," Pete said, thinking he'd better tell her everything at once.

"I plan to take him up to my mother's farm every weekend," she said.

Pete smiled. "Oh he loves to ride in cars!"

Miss Patch began to shuffle through the papers on her desk. She leaned over and handed Pete the wastebasket to empty. Pete took the basket down the hall, emptied it in the large receptacle and came back. Inside the door, he stood a moment watching Miss Patch.

"He rings doorbells," Pete said.

Miss Patch didn't even look up. "The old lady

who lives next door to me is hard of hearing," she said. "She never answers her doorbell."

Pete smiled. He had found a home for Mish at last. He had not only found a home for Mish but he had at one and the same time given Miss Patch the best present she had ever had. She had said so herself! He looked around the room feeling pretty pleased with himself. His glance went from the bulletin board to the blackboard. He decided he liked Room 41. He liked the school and the teacher, and the new home and the new neighborhood. He didn't even mind having Wanda Sparling around — much. He turned to look out the window — and his eyes widened for there pressed against the glass was the face of Wanda. She was waiting for him. He looked at the face squashed against the pane, reflectively. He wondered if he had to tell Miss Patch that Wanda was in it too.

"A little bit of it was Wanda's idea," he said reluctantly because he figured he had to be fair.

"So you and Wanda have become friends!" Miss Patch sounded pleased.

Pete frowned, thinking that when Wanda found out that the teacher liked Mish, she would try to take the glory for herself.

"I would have thought of it myself anyway," Pete assured Miss Patch quickly.

Miss Patch glanced up, looking as if she were holding back a smile. "I'm sure you would have," she said.

Pete hummed as he erased the blackboard. He walked importantly up and down the aisles collecting the work folders from each desk while Miss Patch wrote tomorrow's assignment on the clean blackboard. He pretended not to see Wanda! But when he reached the last desk, he glanced quickly at the teacher's back, and then looked at the face in the window triumphantly.

MOLLY CONE

Molly Cone was born and brought up in Tacoma, Washington, then upon her marriage moved to Seattle, where she, her husband, and their three children now live. She began writing almost as soon as she learned to read, has had articles published in several magazines, and is also the author of previous books, *Only Jane, Too Many Girls* and *The Trouble with Toby*.

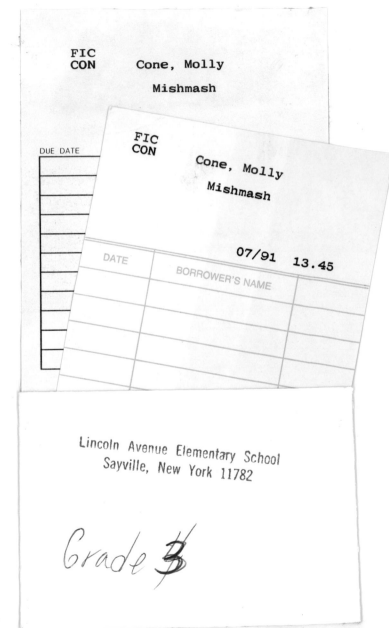

FIC
CON   Cone, Molly

        Mishmash

DUE DATE

FIC
CON   Cone, Molly

          Mishmash

                    07/91   13.45

DATE   BORROWER'S NAME

Lincoln Avenue Elementary School
Sayville, New York 11782

Grade 3